ULTIMATE CRAFTING & RECIPE GUIDE

Learn How to Craft & Build Amazing Things !!!!!

By

Geniuz Gamer

Copyright ©2014 by Geniuz Gamer

Also Discover My Other #1 Bestseller Guides below...

Click on the titles below!

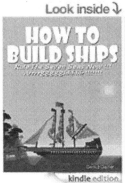
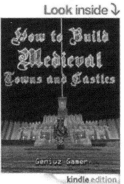

Look inside ↓

Look inside ↓

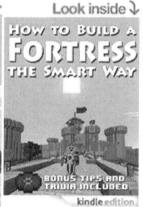

Look inside ↓

Look inside ↓

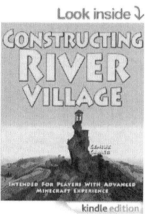

Look inside ↓

Table of Contents

INTRODUCTION

Have you ever wanted to create amazing structures in Minecraft but have no idea how to make them? Or are you a beginner player who doesn't know the first thing about Minecraft but have heard it's a lot of fun from your friends? Or maybe you're a parent who wants to find out how to play Minecraft with your kid? Well this book has all of that, and you'll see for yourself just what you can accomplish through this amazing book.

You'll be taken through the basic stuff you can make in Minecraft to the complex ones that you thought you would never be able to make. It's all laid out in a fun and easy way, and you'll even have pictures to help supplement the text and help you understand it. You can also learn how to enhance your game as well! This is a fun book for any miner who wants to build something bigger than anything they ever expected.

Minecraft is a very fun game and many people have a great time playing it. Players of all ages love to create unique structures that look cool and are also functional. However, many people who start into the game might not know just how much they can build and to what extent. You might want to see the awesome things that you've found online start to come true, and that can be arranged. All you have to do is find the right things and the right facts about various items and start to craft them and then soon you'll have the house and place that everyone will be in envy of.

Or you're one of those new miners who haven't a clue what to do. You might think that one block goes there, and another block goes somewhere else, but then you're left with a home that would even put Picasso to shame. There is a lot to learn in this game, and if you don't have it down pat then you're not going to get far. This book is for you as well, and you can learn the basics in order to become a better miner and challenge yourself to build the biggest and best things that you can.

You might even be one of those miners who want to take their game to the next level. That's right, you might already have it down pat and you want to see just how far you can take it and just how much you can do to it. There is a lot out there that you can do, and some of those things you might not even know about! It's amazing, and you can easily find out how to make the most impressive structures that you can make. It's awesome, and you can take your game to the next level in ways you never even imagined it could go before.

You can do all of these things. From a beginner to an old pro, you can have the best Minecraft experience possible. You can really try out some amazing things, and you can really have a great time in doing it. There is a lot that this game has to offer, but you already know that, and you can definitely find out more of the secrets of this fun game. That's where this book comes in. You'll learn all of the best Minecraft recipe secrets, from the basic things to even the more complex items on the list. There is a lot that you can do, but you might not know just what it could be. You'll go from the most basic of basic information regarding the different blocks and such, and from there you'll learn about the basic structures, and then after that you'll learn about the complex array of materials and things you can craft with this fun and handy game.

This book will teach you some amazing secrets and other things that you will be able to use in your mining game. So sit back, relax, and check out the secrets of Minecraft in this fun and innovative craft & recipe guidebook that can help YOU become even better.

PART ONE:
Basic Tools of the Trade

The first thing you have to know about is the tools of Minecraft. There are a lot out there, and when you see what you have, it might be completely daunting for a second. But don't fret, for you will be able to figure it all out very shortly and you'll be able to understand what they all can do for you. In this handy book you'll find out what each one of them does along with a brief explanation of what you can use it for. This is a great chapter for the beginner miners out there who have just sat down and booted up the game. Don't worry about going crazy over the many different signs and symbols the game has, for once you try it out and you see for yourself just what it does, you won't be able to stop playing and you'll be able to find out more about this fun game.

Wood Planks

This is the basic thing that you'll need in Minecraft. It's how many of the different houses and other structures that you decide to make are built. They may seem small, but they are very important to the game. They're easy to make as well, and the materials are not that hard to procure. They're also key things to use for flooring, pickaxes, and swords. If you want to protect yourself or if you want to mine other blocks besides dirt, you're going to need these.

As you can see, wood planks are easy to make. You won't have to worry about them running out anytime soon. The only disadvantage to them is that they're pretty weak, and unless you're just getting a feel for the game and just want to see what you can make when it comes to basic structures, they're not something you'll be using a lot.

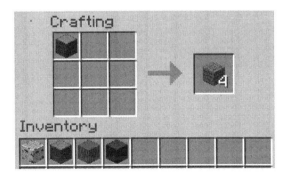

One piece of wood (makes four planks)

Sticks

Sticks are important, but they are a basic weapon as well. All of your mining tools will consist of sticks, and you'll need mining tools to get other blocks in the mines. They are used to craft torches that can help light up areas and are good for when you're in survival mode, and they add an aesthetic value to them as well. They can also make arrows to ward off enemies when you're battling online, and they can be used for fences and signs to help decorate your place. Finally, they can help by being powerful weapons that can help others get the most out of their mining experience. They are also easy to make, and you can decide what you want to do with this fun item. To make it you'll need the following:

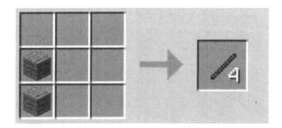

Two wood blocks (makes four sticks)

Torches

This is a great tool to help provide light to the player who's walking around. They're also used in caves to help light the way in the darkest areas. Another great thing these can do for you is help protect you from zombies and undead creatures. These are good basic ways to illuminate the area and help protect you as well. There is more to it than meets the eye, however, as they can also help to melt ice and snow when there is any in the area. If you're in survival mode, then this is integral for you, and you certainly need to have this when you're fighting and trying to carve out the best place to put your epic structure. To make a torch, you need the following:

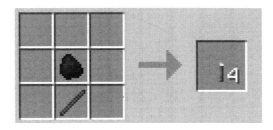

One piece of coal and one stick (makes four torches)

Crafting table

When you are starting out, this is a great way to help you build new items. A crafting table is great for any player who wants to start out building some great things, and it can help you a lot when you're trying to make new weapons. When you start playing, you'll need this in order to create other objects and tools to enhance your game play. To make any furniture structures you're going to need one of these as well. They are also easy to make, and the way to procure the weapons is easy, too. To make it you need the following things:

Four wood planks

Furnace

This is another great basic item to help players make and forge new weapons such as pickaxes, shovels, and axes. Iron is used in these furnaces, and they make stronger weapons and equipment that can help protect you. A furnace can help you with the building aspect of it as well, because you'll need these to make the items to build the house. They are very easy to make, and they have many other great properties as well. You will definitely want to have one of these in your own Minecraft adventures. To make this helpful tool you will need the following:

Eight cobblestones

This will allow you to make new things, and you can help take your game to the next level. It's also integral when you're in survival mode and you need to make new things on the spot without too much time wasted.

Chest

This is another basic thing, but it's very important to have. You can only hold on to so many materials, and you'll soon see that it adds up fast. Your inventory can hold a lot, but when that fills up you won't be able to carry anything else. That turns into a problem when you find something you really want but can't take because of your inventory space. You won't believe it when you see the amount of materials that you'll need not only to build new things, but also to maintain and keep up everything else that you have. You need to have a chest so that you can store the blocks and items that you make, and it can help you a lot and make your Minecraft worries go away. To make it you need the following:

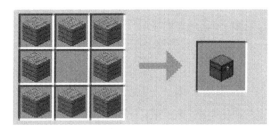

Eight wooden planks

Ladders

A ladder is very important in this game as well, and you will be amazed at the new worlds that you'll be able to make. Have you ever had a house in Minecraft and have you ever wanted to make a two or even a three-story house that will be able to stand upright and without any issues whatsoever? Well, if you have a ladder you'll be able to get up there easily and without any problems at all. With it, you can take your game to a whole new level by giving yourself the ability to make new items to place on the second level. It also allows you to build more rooms and even more detailed things in these structures. It's important to have a ladder, and you will definitely want more than one. Plus, if you're in any terrain or even in survival mode where there might be creepers or other things around and you want to hightail it out of there fast, this is the surefire way to do so without any issues at all. To make it, all you'll need is this:

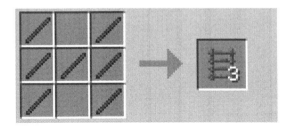

Seven sticks (make three ladders)

Boat

A boat is another underrated thing that you should definitely make if you have the materials. They're easy to craft, and you'll be able to travel on water. With many Minecraft worlds, you'll realize you can go a lot of places but then might become limited because you don't have the transportation to get there. Plus it's easy to get lost in the world of Minecraft, but this will help prevent that. You can work to build your Minecraft structure out into the water, and once you do that, you'll have even more fun things to work with. Plus, if you make a boat you'll be able to check out new and faraway lands, and you'll be able to figure out where you want to make your next structure easily. It's a way to give yourself an even better game with more freedom, and to make it you need the following:

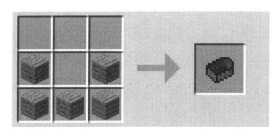

Five wooden planks

Slabs

A slab is something that you might definitely need if you play. When you use a slab, you'll be able to create a gradual slope that's similar to a small hill in the game. You might not know why in the world you need this yet, but when you start to play, you'll soon see why. There are a lot of various types of land that you can have, and if you want to build your structure off a mountain, or if you want to create a way to have your structure going out into the water, then you'll need to do this. It's a very easy way to help you get more land as well, and you can create slopes that gradually go up so that you do not have to worry about getting your Minecraft avatar over a steep incline or anything. To make this helpful tool, you will need the following things:

Two wooden planks make wooden slabs

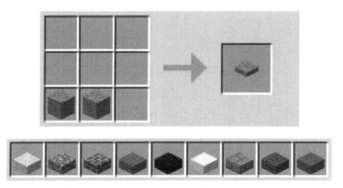

Two stone, brick, sandstone, cobblestone planks (...) make other
kinds of slabs

Doors

A door is a great way not only to add beauty to the house, but it's a great way to protect the house as well. When you're in survival mode, it's one of the key things to have. When a house doesn't have ·it, it'll be subject to zombies and creepers, which can kill you and ruin the structure. If you have it, then nobody will be able to come in unless they have the redstone power. So it's a neat little thing that you can have. A wooden door can be opened by clicking, but if you really want to fortify you'll want to use an iron door. These things are strong, and if you use it then you'll be able to keep your place safe and sound. To make it, you'll simply need the following things:

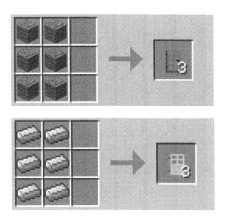

Six wooden planks for three wooden doors, six iron ingots for three iron doors, etc.

These are the basic things to make in order to help you get your foot in the door and work to create some great and wondrous products to help your crafting activities and to help you really get the most out of your Minecraft playing. They're simple to make, and you won't spend a lot of time making these useful tools that can help. This is a great place to start, but in the next couple of chapters you'll find out even more and see for yourself just what you can do with everything.

PART TWO:
Block Recipes

When you're playing Minecraft, you'll want to make sure that you have the helpful blocks as well. Block recipes are things which help you make a certain type of block that can help make the game better. It's extremely important to have these in survival mode, but in basic mode and peaceful mode, you'll be able to use these to help you build strong structures, and they can be used to make bigger houses and even stronger things that can last longer. If you have a knack for building things, or if you want to have the strongest Minecraft house possible, then these are some things that you'll want to check out. They are very simple to make, and all can be used in either peaceful mode or in survival mode.

Glowstone

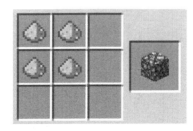

A glowstone is great for nighttime. They are bright, and you'll be able to see them without fail. They can also be used to help you find things that are hard to get, and some of the rare blocks can be found in this fashion. Another way it can be used is for mixing potions, which can help your character get stronger and even more formidable than before. They are very important to make, and you can find glowstone easily in the game. You can usually get it from the glowstone dust that you can obtain either by trading, or by killing witches. To make these glowstones, you will need four glowstone dust.

Snow block

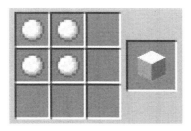

These can help if you're playing your Minecraft game in a cold place. The cold can be fun to build in, and snow blocks can help you create awesome ice structures that look even more amazing when you add other little features to them. They are easy to make as well, and you'll be able to find the materials easily. To make it you'll need four snowballs.

Just as a word of caution, though, if you're not careful and the ice and snow start to melt, this could cause your structures to collapse. So be careful when you're trying to build them, and you'll be able to have an even better time and make even more amazing structures because of it.

Clay block

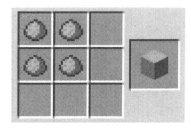

These are helpful because they can be used for storing things by creating clay chests that are strong and hard to break. You can keep all of your great Minecraft tools and other such things in a clay chest, and you'll be able to use them easily and with no issues at all. They are also great to make, and they are strong when it comes to building material, too. It's something that you'll definitely need, and you can help take your game to the next level with them. To make it all you need is four pieces of clay.

Brick block

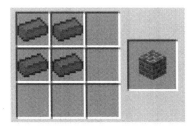

A brick block is a great way to help you build even more things. They are strong, so they can be used as a great foundation and they can be used to help fortify structures so that they don't get pushed down when others try to attack. It's important to have, and you'll be able to easily make them without any issues. They are something that will help any miner who wants to help make strong structures that can hold a lot, and you won't have to worry about everything coming tumbling down because of it. To make these epic structures you'll need four bricks per block.

Bookcase

A bookcase looks cool in a Minecraft house. There isn't a whole lot you can do with it, but you might want one to help decorate the home. Plus, you might get to find some cool books as well, and they can help to decorate the shelf even more. Even though they don't help when it comes to defense, they are still impressive and it is something that many miners like to have as an extra added decoration to their place. To make it you'll need six wooden planks and three books.

Sandstone block

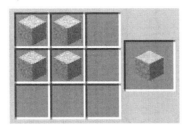

Sandstone blocks are great to have, and they can help to build more structures that are on the pretty side. You might want to have strong things, but if you're the type that also wants a hint of decoration in their Minecraft structures, then this is the way to go. It's not as strong as brick, but it does hold up pretty well when it comes to building things, and you'll see how well it does when you use it. It's also very easy to make, and you can even make them with the sand that you find on the beaches of the game. To make one you will need four pieces of sand.

Note block

If you want to leave notes for others and you want to let others know what you're doing when you're playing online or with friends offline, then this is something that can be helpful to make and something that you can use. It's helpful for those who want to try out new things in the game, and they don't require a whole lot of skill to make. To craft this you will need eight wooden planks surrounding one redstone.

Jack O'Lantern

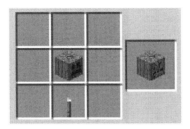

When Halloween comes to Minecraft, this can be a great and spooky way to show off your love for a fun holiday. Not only does it look good and fit with the festivities of the season, you can use it as a very valuable light source that can help you find everything that you need at night. If you want to go exploring you can use this as well. To make this helpful tool you'll need one pumpkin and one torch.

Stairs

If you're the type to have stairs in your place instead of ladders, then these are for you. The stairs are great for when you want to go up and down, and you'll be able to easily make them. They are also good if you're the kind who wants to give your home an easy route in and out, and if you want to add them to the outside of the home, you'll be able to do so as well. To make them you'll need six wooden planks (for wood stairs) or cobblestone, sandstone, brick, stone, etc. to make four stairs.

Stained Clay

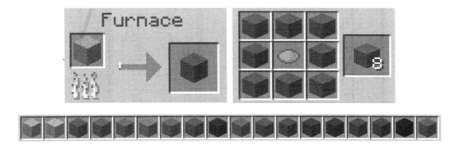

Are you the type who likes to have pretty clay structures in Minecraft? Do you want to decorate your place a little bit and give it a very nice makeover that you'll love and the kind that your friends will wonder how you did? Well then, this is for those who want to have a pretty and decorative color to the house, and it works as a great building material. It's strong, and you'll be able to use it to fortify your place so that you can prevent anyone from coming by and taking it down. To make it you'll need eight pieces of hardened clay and one dye.

Hay bale

This is a fun item for those who want to take care of animals and those who want to have fun making some of their Minecraft structures. It's a great way to feed your horses too, and you won't have to worry about spending any money or other such things taking care of them. They look nice, too, and you'll be able to put them around your structure to give it a pretty feel and to make it look amazing. To make it you'll simply need nine pieces of wheat.

All of these structures are easy to make and add a bit of flair to your place. This takes your game to a whole new level, and it can help you when you're trying to make bigger and better structures. These can be used for defense as well if you're playing that mode of the game. But what about actually making big and huge things, and how are you supposed to make them? Well, in the next chapter you'll learn how to build some of the cool Minecraft structures that are out there, and this is good for those who already know the basics and want to find out more about the different things that one can make in this fun game.

PART THREE:
How to Build Big Structures

Now that you know about the small things that you want to make, it's time to bring out the big guns and see how you can make the bigger Minecraft structures. These are basic, but they do require some time and effort to make them. It's not very hard, but you might have to take a bit of time to make them. Here are some helpful tips on how to make the cool Minecraft structures that are not too insane just yet. Don't worry, the crazy ideas are in the next chapter and they are something that you will not want to miss and something that you will definitely want to try out for yourself.

The Cube

For those who are just starting, this is something that you will want to have. It's not that hard to make, but it doesn't have a whole lot of space either. When you first play the game, this is the first thing you're going to make. It can only hold a bed, a couple of the furnaces, and a crafting table. This is a way to get you started, but you don't want to limit yourself to just that. To make this epic structure you'll need only wood.

First, start off with making an 8x8 structure on three sides. This will make the three faces of the house.

Next, do the same with the other side, but take out two of the blocks. That will leave room for the door.

Add a door in the open area.

Use the same dimensions to finish off the house with a roof.

Once you make it, you'll have a small house that you can use to build up on.

The Castle

This is another very small structure to make, and it's something that you will want to try out. Don't think it's one of those big and crazy castles that you've seen in the past, because it's not. These castles are just simple little cubes that come with snipers and cannons. They are good for those who are playing in survival mode and those who want to try out their hand at putting a sort of defensive measure up in their structures. To make it you'll need the same ingredients as in the cube above, and the snipers and cannons can be added to it as well for an even more interesting effect. To build it, follow the instructions below.

For a simple one, make the same shape you did with the cube house but take out two blocks to make windows and two blocks on the bottom to make doorways.

Do that for each side, and then on each corner of the top put a wood block on top.

Attach torches wherever you want.

You can add a moat by digging a hole and filling it with water using a bucket. You can do this with lava as well. Just make sure to put a block down before you cross.

Freestanding house

This is a basic house that's all out there, and they are good for those who are just starting. If you're playing in survival mode, this might not be the house or structure that you're going to want to keep, for they are very easy to spot and they can be very out in the open. However, you can have multiple floors with this, and you'll be able to gather and make even more complex structures because of this later on. To build it, follow the instructions below.

First you dig a 10x10 hole to make the floor. Then fill that with wood planks.

After, build a wall around it about 6 blocks high. Add in a ceiling as well along with roofing tools.

You can add windows if desired by cutting out a 2x2 block hole.

Add other amenities such as torches, beds, etc.

House in a Cave

If you're the type who doesn't want to have to deal with building a whole bunch of new stuff yet, then this might be perfect for you. You might get a cave that Minecraft gives to you, and you'll be able to check it out and make it your home for a while. There are other natural structures out there, and you can use those as well. To make them, however, you will need some pickaxes, and those might cost many materials and might take a lot of time to make. If you're the type who wants to have more of a natural home, but you're willing to sacrifice the pickaxes and the time it might take to make it, then go for it. You might want to have a landmark as well, for it's easy to get these places mixed up on the server, and you don't want to have that happen. To make these houses, you'll have to do this:

-acquire at least 2 pickaxes

-find a landmark

-dig it out

-use wood and wool to make a bed

-add in the bed, bookshelf, crafting table, etc.

As a word of caution however, make sure that you don't have it anywhere bad guys can get to you. These are better to build in creative mode rather than survival mode. If you do build it in survival mode, make sure you fortify it to protect yourself.

Lean-to

For those who are willing to try out something else and who want to put a bit more effort into their building, this is for you. These are kind of like a hybrid house, part of it freestanding and another part resting on a natural structure. It's a way to combine the best parts of both worlds, and they are fun to make. You can put it against a cave or other structure, and they can be ideal for those who want to take their houses underground, plus they are very easy to make. To do this, you will need:

-a natural structure (can be inside or outside)

-some wood or stone blocks to make part of the house and the roof. Usually, making it an 8x8 structure on each side plus a door works.

-pickaxes if you want to expand your house underground to improve its structure and awesomeness

Space Needle

The name of this means what it says. This is a structure that is a house at the bottom with a point going up it leading to some crazy height. This is a fun one for those who like to have something a bit different, and something that will surely make others not want to attack you. If you're the kind who wants to prevent creepers from coming to destroy everything, then this is perfect for you. They have great views and you can even build other structures on top of it if you're willing to do so. The only thing that is bad about them is that they take forever to make, and it might bore you to death. They cost a ton of resources as well. If you're not willing to put the effort into making it, then this might not be for you. However, if you want a cool structure you can definitely make it, and you will be able to do so by looking at these items and directions:

-obtain about 500 blocks of either wood or stone. You might not need all of that, but it's helpful

-grab some paper and think about how you want your design to be

-put the mainframe of the house together at the bottom. Make a simple structure of slabs and stone walls, then make the base before making the huge needle going up

-make the needle, making sure that it has a thick bottom and then allowing it to taper all the way up

-at the top, put a few slabs of either wood or stone to create a place to stand, or make a small structure such as a house or a small cube house

-check out the view and enjoy your house!

The Framed Tower

This is another simple structure that can be used to make even bigger ones. You can also manipulate this in order to make Tudor-style houses so that you can have a little bit more variety in your Minecraft building. They are pretty simple, and you can make the structure with both wood and cobblestone, so you won't have to look very far for the materials in order to get them. They are also pretty cool, and you can even switch out some of the wood for logs so that you can add even more variety to your home. To make this very simple but effective structure, all you need to do is the following.

-make 4-5 block towers with cobblestone or with a stone material (make sure that it's strong)

-arrange all of these in either a square or rectangle.

-put cobblestone beams up at the top of it to join each of these.

-you can add more by filling in the gaps with wooden planks that are easy to join together

-next, add the roof by putting wooden planks all over it

-place stairs in there as well to access the roof if

you want

-if you want a unique roof, place wooden stairs at the top instead of wooden planks, putting them in a pitched fashion with different sizes.

-finally, add windows if you so desire, and then you have your simple house that works really well.

Underground shelter

If you're familiar with the infamous bomb shelters that are around in real life, then you might have heard of this one. It's a bomb shelter that can be used as a nonpublic shelter for your character. These are good when you're playing in safe mode, but it also can be effective in survival mode. The main thing with this one is you need to make sure you don't lose it, and that you also put it in an ideal location instead of willy-nilly. With this one, you have to watch out for lakes or lava, because if that is around that can be a big problem for you, and you're more at risk of dying because of it. However, if you do desire to have a shelter like this, it can also work to your advantage, for you'll be able to hide from enemies better and you'll be able to have better protection. The major disadvantage, however, is you won't be able to see outside, so be careful and smart when you're planning these structures. To do this you will need the following and have to do the following things.

-first, you can figure out where to put your place by marking it with either a sign or a torch. A torch might hold up better, so it's highly recommended

-next, start to use a shovel and pickaxe in order to dig and build your shelter

-add in lighting such as lamps and other such things so that you're able to see effectively

-next, you will want to put some stairs in there. Make sure it's discreet, though, and not completely out in the open

-if you're willing to take the risk, you can put a hole there in order to help you see out, or you can even arrange a window as well. But be careful when you do this, and if you're in survival mode, it's even more important.

Half-house

This is a house that's a sort of hybrid of both an underground and a normal house. It's different from a lean-to because it's partially above and partially below ground. These can be great if you need to hide and make a quick getaway, but it does have its disadvantages as well. For example, you want to make sure that it's in a location that isn't out in the open, because if a creeper comes around and blows up your house, you might get damaged as well. The one big advantage is that if you do get blown up, you'll still have a structure to run to after the damage is done. To build one you will need to do the following:

-find a location that's both easy to hide and also able to accommodate what you need it for

-start to dig a hole with some of the shovels and pickaxes that you have, making a small underground place

-add in the light in order to see effectively

-put in whatever else you want in your Minecraft home

-add in some stairs to go out

-next, build your house. You can do a simple structure, or you can do a framed structure.

That's all based on your preference, and you should go off of that

-finally, add a door and windows and then you're done!

Farms

Farms seem very generic, but you can add your own personal flair to them. They can be fun, and if you're into farming you can get the farming mod to add a bit to it. You can get some animals, and this could be an extra challenge as well. It's hard to keep a farm in survival mode, but if you're game for it then it's definitely worth a shot and something you might want to undertake. To make a farm you can do the following

-start off with a bunch of wood blocks. Make a rectangular shape similar to a farmhouse. You can make it big or small depending on personal tastes

-next, make the roof by adding first a set of wood planks on the bottom, and then putting in stairs in order to make a pitched roof that looks similar to a farmhouse roof

-if you have the ability to dye the blocks, you can dye it to your personal preference color. If you want red, you can do that

-next, make a small pen for the chickens by putting about three wood blocks by two wood blocks.

-get some chickens and put them in there

-you can add other animals as well

-to make a main house for your farm, you can either do it as a simple house, or you can make it into your own personal unique structure

-after that, you can have fun farming and taking care of animals!

Structures in the sky

Minecraft has the fun and unique ability to allow you to build things up in the air. That's right, if you want to have fun and build things high in the sky you totally can. Plus, if you're playing in survival mode you can definitely hide from creepers and others in this fashion. Some have even taken it to the next level and built these huge and impressive sky fortresses that look great and amaze many people. They are pretty easy to make, and there are very few limitations, but you do have to be a creative person in order to do this. To make this you have to do the following:

-first, figure out where you're going to build it

-next, make a foundation out of wood blocks and slabs to hold the house.

-then, build the house on top of it

-you can add designs such as the needle to it once you're done

-this one might be a bit hard for those who aren't creative enough with Minecraft designs just yet, but if you need some assistance when it comes to designing things, simply sketch them out on a piece of paper. It may help you in many ways and it can do wonders for your creativity as well.

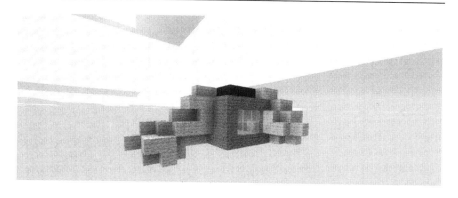

All of these are some of the simple structures that one can start off with. They are easy, and you'll be able to use them in order to create amazing things and impress your friends in the world of Minecraft.

PART FOUR:
Furniture for your Crib and other Amenities

The basic structures can be fun, but then there are other things to look into as well. That is the furniture, the way you decorate the place to make it look amazing. There is a lot that you can do with a place like that, and you can certainly create a whole lot more from these basic things. In this chapter you will learn how to build the awesome things that can help make a home in Minecraft the place that it's supposed to be.

Fireplace

A fireplace can really help your avatar during the wintertime and it's something that a lot of houses have. Plus, they can look cool with the right things around them, and adding torches and lava in it can make the structure more than meets the eye. To make this sort of structure, you will need to do these things

-obtain about 10-50 bricks, depending on size

-start with six on each side, each of them going up

-Add a beam of bricks up at the top to make the mantel piece

-Next, add a flue by putting it up the wall of the house. This can be either one block wide, or up to two less than the width of the fireplace

-to add more to it, put a lava block inside to start a fire

-as a decorative extra, you can even put two torches on top to help decorate the place even more.

Chairs

Chairs are a great way to help make your house more livable and a lot prettier. There is a lot that you can do with these things, and if you want to you can even create a couch out of these. They are great to put around the house, and if your character wants to get off his feet he can. To make them, you have to do the following:

-place one stair block on the bottom to make the seat

-add two signs on either side

-to make a couch, you can extend the seat by 2-4 blocks, depending on how long you want it to be.

Desks and counters

These two things go hand in hand, and they are a great extension of the tables that you know how to make. They can help decorate a house, and including a desk and chair set in a home can give it a studious look. You can even make a stone desk if you desire by using the right materials. To make these do the following:

-for the counters, all you have to do is put a bunch of wood blocks next to each other to the distance that you want them to be

-to make the desks, take a couple of the tables and arrange them in a horizontal fashion. That makes the main part of the desk

-if you want it to jut out a little, simply put either one or two tables on each end of it to create an office desk

-add a chair and then you're done!

Fountains

You might not believe it, but you can build fountains in your Minecraft world. They are pretty cool, and you can put them in or out of a home. This can make any structure look pretty, and others will marvel at the amazing thing that you've created. There are a couple of ways to make them, but this is the simplest one out there.

-first, you dig a hole in the ground in a circular shape. You can also do a 5x5 square if you want a square fountain. The size doesn't matter as long as it's dug

-next, add stones around the perimeter in order to create a barrier. You should do them about two blocks high

-after that, build a pillar of stone in the center. You can build a few more around as well

-at the top, add a stone plank cut into any shape you want it to be

-finally, add the water into the hole and then you have a beautiful fountain that you can be proud of!

Beds

A bed can help make a house pretty interesting, and you can add it as a nice addition. Plus, you can even sleep on it if you so desire, and it's a great addition to any Minecraft home that you make. They aren't too hard to make, either, and it's a great piece to have. To make one, you have to do the following:

-put four blocks of wood at the bottom to make the base of it

-put wooden slabs on top

-add a blanket and pillow as well

-then you have a bed you can use and it will be the perfect addition to any structure that you make.

All of these things are great additions to any

home or structure that you make, and you can impress your friends with these while you're learning to build some new and other cool things that will look great!

PART FIVE:
Tools to take the game to the next level

When you're playing Minecraft, you want to try out new things. You want to be one of those players that can build insane homes and other such structures. That's a lot of fun to do, but it can be hard work. However, there is a way to prepare everything before you actually start to work on it, so that you don't waste time if you mess up in any way. Plus, you can actually learn a lot from using these things. Here are the top six ways to help take your Minecraft game to the next level in an easy and effective way.

Minedraft

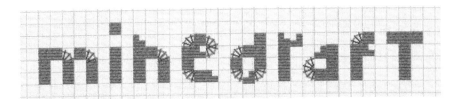

The name may sound familiar, but it's more than just a tool. This is a thing that you can use to help plan your structures before you build them so that you can make sure that you don't mess up and can keep everything in the right order. Think about the blueprints that some architects use; they can be huge, and that's similar to what happens in Minecraft. Minedraft, however, allows you to make up everything for the structure before you do it, and you can use these plans. It's a great way to plan everything before you take on big and scarier structures, and you can also save yourself the headache as well.

Worldpainter

This is similar to when some comic book creators use MS Paint or other such things in order to help them make things before they do them. This tool allows you to plan out your Minecraft maps without any issues through the use of MS Paint. You can then put them into the game immediately to use them, so you won't have to worry about the problems of transferring it and the fear of messing up horrendously. It's a very nifty tool that can help you build the cities that you want to, and it's integral to have if you're itching to build either a city or a ton of structures on a piece of land.

Building Inc.

Let's say that you see something cool online. It's something that you really want to make. However, you don't have the skills as of yet to make something as cool as this, and you don't know how to start. The skills might be too much for a beginner, but there is a way to make these things. With this tool you'll be able to recreate some of the cool structures that you see. You can see how they did it, and with that you'll be able to make your own things easily and with less of a headache. You can see how they're made, and from there you can work to hone your own skills so that you can build even more epic things quickly and with great results as well.

Mods

Mods can help you change the game a lot. If you want to see just how different the game can be with them, then you should try them out. They are all available online, but you should make sure that the site is safe before you download them. They can change the game by allowing you to change the texture of a few buildings or other structures. You can also add other tools and types of blocks as well if you find different mods, and this can help you change the game that you have. You can also talk to other people online who might have the same building issues as you, and you two can trade mods and other such tips in order to help each other have the best game possible

Good Old Pencil and Paper

Did you know that Minecraft can be educational and can help you understand some aspects of math better? Well, it can, and that's how it can be used when it comes to making epic Minecraft structures. You can even cut out the plans and put them around you in order to help you get motivated to make the structure that you desire to create in the game.

You start out by doing a basic sketch of how many blocks you want something to be and build your structures on the blocks of graph paper. If you want something bigger, you can buy bigger blocks from the store and use architecture paper to help with that.

Then, you can sketch it out and make your designs come true in the game. It's a simple, cheap, and effective way, and if you're not the type to want to make huge 3D models on the computer or if you're not very technology savvy, then this is good for you.

All of these things can help you with your Minecraft experience, and it's a great way to help you get the most out of your Minecraft playing. It's also great to use before you start, and with this you can save yourself from any unnecessary stress and worry later on. Don't stress yourself out while you play your favorite game, plan ahead and you will be fine.

PART SIX:
The REAL Challenges

Now that you've learned a lot about the basics, it's time to take your game to the next level. You might have practiced a lot, and a lot of those structures can be daunting. However, after you've mastered them you might want to figure out how to take your game to the next level. It's simple, and you can do a whole lot with this. Plus, if you start from here, you can build up on it and learn some even more cool techniques. In this chapter you will find out about some of the other epic things you can do in Minecraft, and you'll even get tutorials on how to make some of the more complex structures out there so you can impress your friends and have even more fun as a result.

Lighthouses

A lighthouse is something that can be used not only to help you find your way, but they can be fun to make as well. You will want to have a lot of material to do this, and you can definitely have a lot of fun making these things. If you really want to, you can build even more things on top of it, but this will be just the basic steps on how to make a lighthouse.

-first, figure out where you are. That sounds pretty simple, but location is everything for a structure like this. You don't want to botch this up, and the best locations are either by a body of water or in the middle of an island to help you figure out where you are. It's also a great landmark to use when you're trying to find a place, and it can be a way to help you demarcate your city as well.

-after that, start doing pillar jumping to make a tower using cobblestone.

-once you're at the right height, start to place down some of the slabs to help you create a balcony to stand on

-make sure to leave a hole, however, so you can climb up if you want to

-after that, build a small tower on top of it with cobblestone

-at the top of it, you can put either a torch, a glowstone, or a redstone to help illuminate the structure

-to get up there, you should fall down and move against it, placing ladders all around to the top of it.

-after that, you can attach clocks to note blocks to help you find out what time it is.

Lava Pillar

This is a different type of tower that can help you illuminate the way. This might be a bit easier to see in the daytime and during the night, but it might require more materials. Plus you should also be wary of location because it is made of lava. The directions to make this are as follows

-dig a 4x4x1 hole and make sure that there are walls all around

-make a pillar two blocks away from the center out of sand or of flimsy wood

-Once you have the height that you want it to be, put a walkway to the center out of slabs

-destroy the connecting block over the center of

the pillar

-put the lava on top of the center block to destroy the outer pillar. Make sure that you're out of the way as well in case the lava touches you

-you can add to this by building glass walls around the lava pillar for extra protection.

Wood House

A wood house is a bit more complex than the basic house, and you can do a lot with it. Plus, you can build other stories and other amenities as well. They are very functional, and work wonders as well. To build a wood house, you need to do the following steps:

-first you dig an 8x12 hole and fill it with wood planks. Make sure not to make more than one layer

-then, cover the edge with wood, but leave a gap so that you can put a door on

-add glass wherever you desire to create windows, and then fill in the rest with wood to create the structure

-place wood planks over it to create a roof, making sure to put one extra block over the edge

-you can add a second floor by doing the same with the wood blocks and wood planks, adding windows as needed

Tree House

A tree house can be fun to make, and the structure can be complex. You can start off with this, and you can build on it from there. To make this you can do the following:

-first, build a tower of blocks 4x4 going all the way up to the desired height

-next, determine where you want the landings to be, and once you've decided create the area by placing wooden slabs all the way around it, leaving a little bit of room for the stairs

-start to place a layer of wood blocks on the slabs to help create the house structure

-leave out two spaces to put the doors in

-add glass blocks as needed to create windows

-finish by putting slabs at the top and make sure to add the doors in as well

-the last step is to add a ladder to get in and out of it, and after that you can put a fence around the general area as well to help block off the edges and keep yourself from falling off.

Castle

A castle is a pretty complex thing, and you might not get it right on your first try. But it's worth a shot, and these steps will help you be able to do that easily, and without any issues whatsoever. It's also a great fortress to make in order to protect yourself, and you'll see just how awesome it can be after you build it. To make this, you'll need to do the following steps:

-first, plan out where you're going to make it. This isn't some small thing, it's a giant thing that might take a lot of time and a whole lot of effort. Make sure you assess the area before making a decision

-next, terraform the location in order to clear it out and get rid of some of the trees and hills

-next, build an entire wall around the area and show what you need to enclose

-then, plan where you're going to put everything before doing so

-next, build up the outer wall to whatever height you want it to be. You can change it around and tape it if you want to

-next, add a tower of stone blocks at each intersection, leaving out a set of three holes on each side to create places to see out of To build up a tower, put blocks going all the way up in a square, putting stairs in so you can get up to it. You can add floors every so often, and you can build it to a very high level

-once done, you can change the materials every so often and add the details to make it look better, such as sandstone or other materials

-you can build more towers around, adding in glass walls and other things to your liking. You can even do little niches in each of the tower tops by making every other block higher than the one next to it

-finally, build the entrance where you want by deciding where it's going to go. Then, make sure that it's a bit wider than everywhere else, and you can even put stairs leading up to it as well. Finally, decide on the doorway by either leaving it open or putting a portcullis at the entrance to help guard it. Make sure you know how to use a redstone first before doing that

Ship

Ships are another complex structure that can be cool and unique in the Minecraft world. They also are good protection, because you can leave and live on the water if there is an attack from other people. However, they do take time to build and they might take a long time. These steps will tell you how to build it, however, and once you start you won't want to stop.

-the first thing you have to do is plan it so that you know just how you want it to look. Do you want it to be square? Or do you want it to be anther shape? Make sure you have it planned out.

-next, put blocks in a row on the middle of the ship. Start building it up with 1 block every 3-5 blocks until about halfway and then do one block for every 1-2 blocks until you've reached the desired height.

-after that, build it outwards starting from one side to the desired width of the boat. Make sure it isn't too wide. Usually about 8-11 blocks from the middle works, but it also depends upon the type of ship that you're building

-after that, start tapering it out by putting one block for every two blocks each place. Then you do the same to the other side until you have both sides of the ship built out

-to make the front look good, you will have to experiment by adding and removing blocks until it looks the same. Work with different types of blocks so that it looks better that way. Obviously it won't be 100% smooth, but it does the job

-to do the back, create an anchor shape and build it from there, trimming it off as necessary. The shape will look odd, but remember that it will be in the water

-after, add on the layers of blocks, adding windows when you want, until you have it at the desired size. You can also leave one side bigger to create a room within the ship

-for the hull, just create a long line of blocks and then tweak them to make sure that it looks good

-after, you can add a sail by making a long column of blocks about 10 blocks wide and then making it bigger as you go back and then extending it out onto one side. It might take a while, but you'll get it

-finally, add planks and stairs to make floors and then you have a boat

---

These structures may take a bit more time, but they can really impress others and you'll be amazed yourself at all of the awesomeness that you have created and the skills that you have now.

CONCLUSION

Minecraft is a ton of fun, and you can learn to build new and impressive things with it. There is a lot that you can do with this, and you can work to take your game to a whole new level. This is a start to the many things that you can make in the world of Minecraft, and you'll soon see what you can do with it once you start to play it.

The next thing to do is to go out there, use what you've learned in this book, and then have fun with it. Just try out all these things, and you'll soon see what you can do with the game. If you have any questions you can always write a review, or you can even try hard and figure it out yourself. Remember you are an awesome Minecraft player and you can make amazing things!

Now all that's left is to turn on the game, open it up, and have some serious fun making things in this great game filled with a whole bunch of challenges.

Thank you so much for reading my book. I hope you enjoyed it.

If you liked the book, **would you please take a moment** to leave a review?

It would mean the world to me :))))

Thank you so much!!!!

p.s. for more guides or stories, please check my author page Geniuz Gamer :)))

Made in the USA
San Bernardino, CA
19 May 2018